I0702166

For America Hope

There once was a little bird named Nightin, a
Nightingale that lived with her Mommy Gale
in a tall, tall tree.

This Nightingale was small and not very tall, but she was full of curiosity.

Nightin watched as other gales in the forest flew through the blue sky. And she wanted nothing more than to also feel her wings through the breeze.

"Can you teach me how to fly?" Nightin asked Mommy Gale. But Mommy Gale only sighed. "Your wings are too small, and you aren't very tall. One day I'll teach you to fly. But not now, not now at all."

Nightin was very sad to hear she was not tall and that her wings were too small. For little Nighten was desperate to learn to fly, fly, fly.

But day by day, and week by week,
Nightin began to grow, little by little,
bit by bit.

"Please, teach me to fly," Nightin asked Mommy Gale again, but Mommy Gale only sighed.

"Your wings are too small and you aren't very tall. One day I'll teach you to fly. But not now, not now at all."

Nightin was sad, because she felt she had grown. But it just wasn't enough. She still wasn't tall, and her wings still far too small. She couldn't yet learn to fly, fly, fly.

But little Nightin was undeterred.
Night by night, and month by
month, Nightin continued to grow,
little by little, bit by bit.

"Can you teach me how to fly?" Nightin asked Mommy Gale. "You see, my wings are not small. I've grown quite tall. Please, Mommy Gale, teach me how to fly, fly, fly."

"Dear little Nightin, I think it's time. Your wings are
not small, you've grown quite tall. Now, follow me
to the end of the tree."

Nightin followed her mother to the end of the tree, feeling only a little scared as she was told to spread her wings.

"Jump real high, and spread your wings wide. Then flap them real fast like the strong bird you are, and you'll be able to fly, fly, fly".

Nightin spread her wings and flapped them really fast,
then jumped oh so high from the edge of the tree.

Flap, flap, flap...

Jump, jump, jump...

Nightin flew, flew, flew over the trees, far to the edge of the forest, smiling with glee. Turning at the end and flying right back again, she landed with her Mommy Gale in the tall, tall tree.

"I did it! I did it!" Nightin sang happily. "I flew through the forest and back to our tree, Mommy Gale, Mommy Gale! Did you see?"

"I saw you Nightin. You did amazing!
I'm so very proud you learned to fly, fly, fly."

That was when Nightin saw tears in Mommy Gale's eyes, and she wondered why she had started to cry, cry, cry.

"Time went by so fast, in the blink of an eye. And now that you know how to fly, fly, fly, I'm worried you'll be saying goodbye, bye, bye."

Nightin loved her Mommy Gale and their cozy nest too. She never wanted to leave, even though she could now soar through the sky so blue.

"Don't worry, Mommy Gale. I promise that even though I know how to fly, fly, fly, I'll always come back to you. I'll never say goodbye, bye, bye."

About The Author

Kendra Thomas is from Mapleton Utah, a small town pressed against the beautiful Rocky Mountains. Kendra has been an aspiring author since she was in sixth grade. She has a passion for fairy tales and romantasy books.

Along with songwriting, horse riding, and playing the guitar, Kendra Thomas is a Dental Hygienist by day and a writer by night. She earned her bachelor's degree at the Utah College of Dental Hygiene at the young age of nineteen years old. She is also happily married to her best friend, Cade Thomas, and together they have a beautiful daughter, America Hope.

Her most wanted dream is for others to love her stories and characters as much as she cherishes them. She hopes to inspire other young authors to pursue their dreams, and to write about the worlds inside their heads as she was once inspired to do as a young girl. She hopes that her books might be a place of sanctuary for those seeking a whimsical getaway and a thrilling adventure.